Ruben's Race Car

Story by Cameron Macintosh
Illustrations by Dusan Lakicevic

Contents

Chapter 1

A Solar-Powered Watch

It was Friday morning.
Ruben was enjoying his favourite subject, science.
Mr Tamura was telling the class about solar power.

"You might have noticed my solar watch before," said Mr Tamura.
"It has a solar panel behind the clock hands, so I never have to wind it or put a new battery in it. Come and have a look."

Mr Tamura placed the watch on his desk.
Everybody came up and looked at it closely.

Ruben admired it more than anyone.
"I've seen solar panels on houses," he said,
"but I've never seen one on a watch!"

"If you look around, you'll be surprised how often
you see solar panels," said Mr Tamura.
"There are even solar-powered cars and buses."

"How does your watch work?" asked Ruben.

"The sunlight hits the solar panel behind the hands on my watch," explained Mr Tamura. "Then the panel changes the energy from the sunlight into electricity. The electricity is stored in the watch's battery."

"So that's how it works!" said Ruben.

"Yes," said Mr Tamura. "We can use the sun's energy in all sorts of ways."

SOLAR
CELL
BATTERY

Chapter 2

Racetrack Troubles

The next day, Ruben had his friend Max over to play.

"Let's race your remote-controlled cars," said Max.

"Great idea!" replied Ruben.

Ruben and Max went into the backyard to set up a racetrack. They made a jump using rocks and pieces of wood, and soon had the perfect track.

"Let's race!" said Ruben.

The boys had a great time racing the cars.

They had won a race each
when Ruben's car suddenly stopped moving,
just as it approached the jump.

He ran over to pick it up.

"The batteries have run out," he moaned. "I'll go inside and find some new ones."

Ruben went inside and looked in the box
where the extra batteries were usually kept.
But this time there were no batteries there.

Ruben ran to see Mum.
"Mum, I've run out of batteries for my car!" he said.
"Can you please take Max and me to the shops
to get some new ones?"

"Sorry, Ruben," Mum replied.
"I need to finish a lot of work before 4 o'clock.
We can probably go tomorrow."

Disappointed, Ruben and Max played video games until Max's mum came to get him later that afternoon.

When Ruben went to bed that night, he was still unhappy that he had not been able to keep racing his car.

But as he lay in bed, he had an exciting idea.

Chapter 3

Ruben's Idea

The next morning, Ruben asked Mum to help him send an email to the company that had made his remote-controlled car.

They sat down together at Mum's computer. Ruben typed all the words he'd been thinking before he had fallen asleep last night.

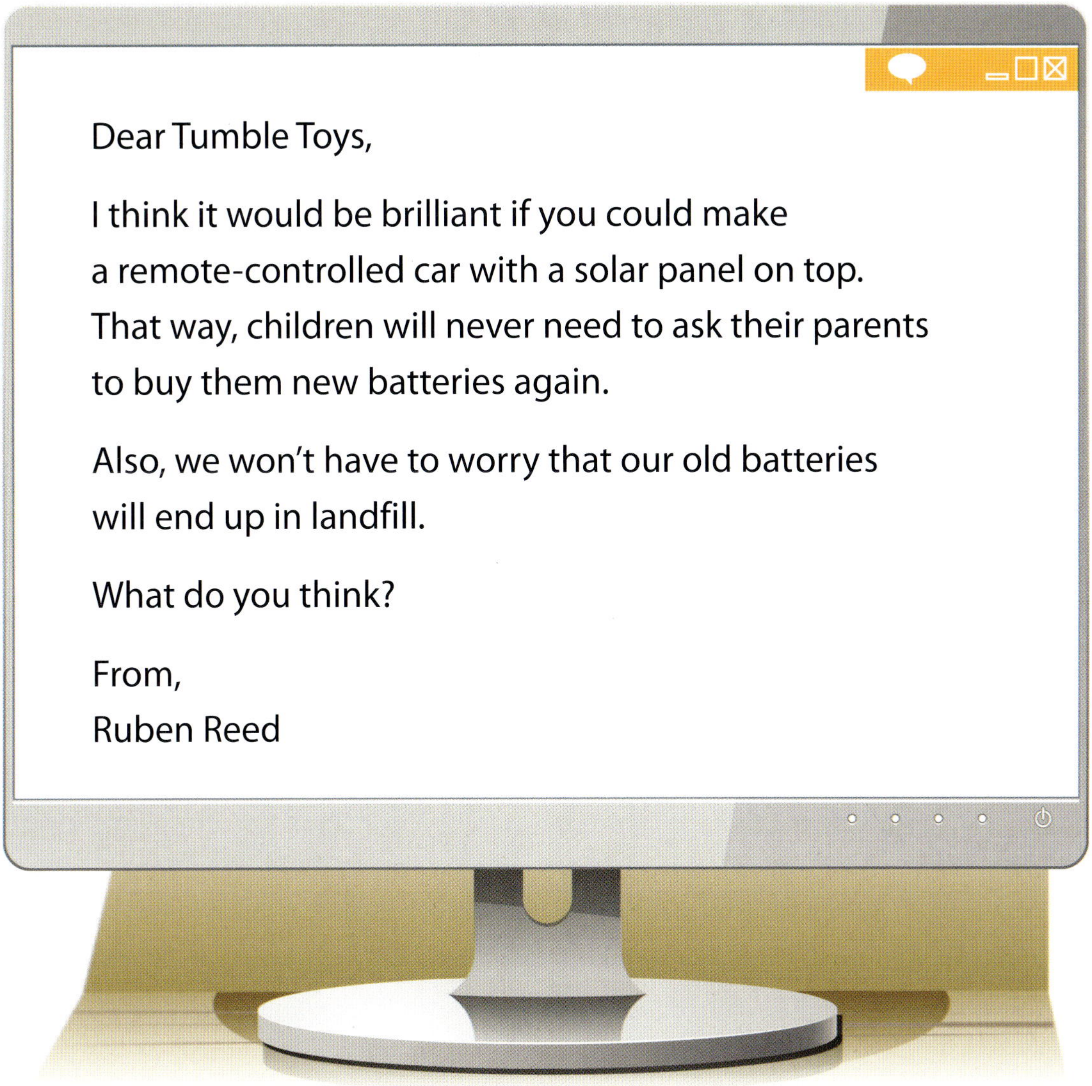

Dear Tumble Toys,

I think it would be brilliant if you could make a remote-controlled car with a solar panel on top. That way, children will never need to ask their parents to buy them new batteries again.

Also, we won't have to worry that our old batteries will end up in landfill.

What do you think?

From,
Ruben Reed

Ruben sent the email, then went to make breakfast.

Ruben didn't really think he would hear back from Tumble Toys, but on Wednesday morning, there was an email for him.

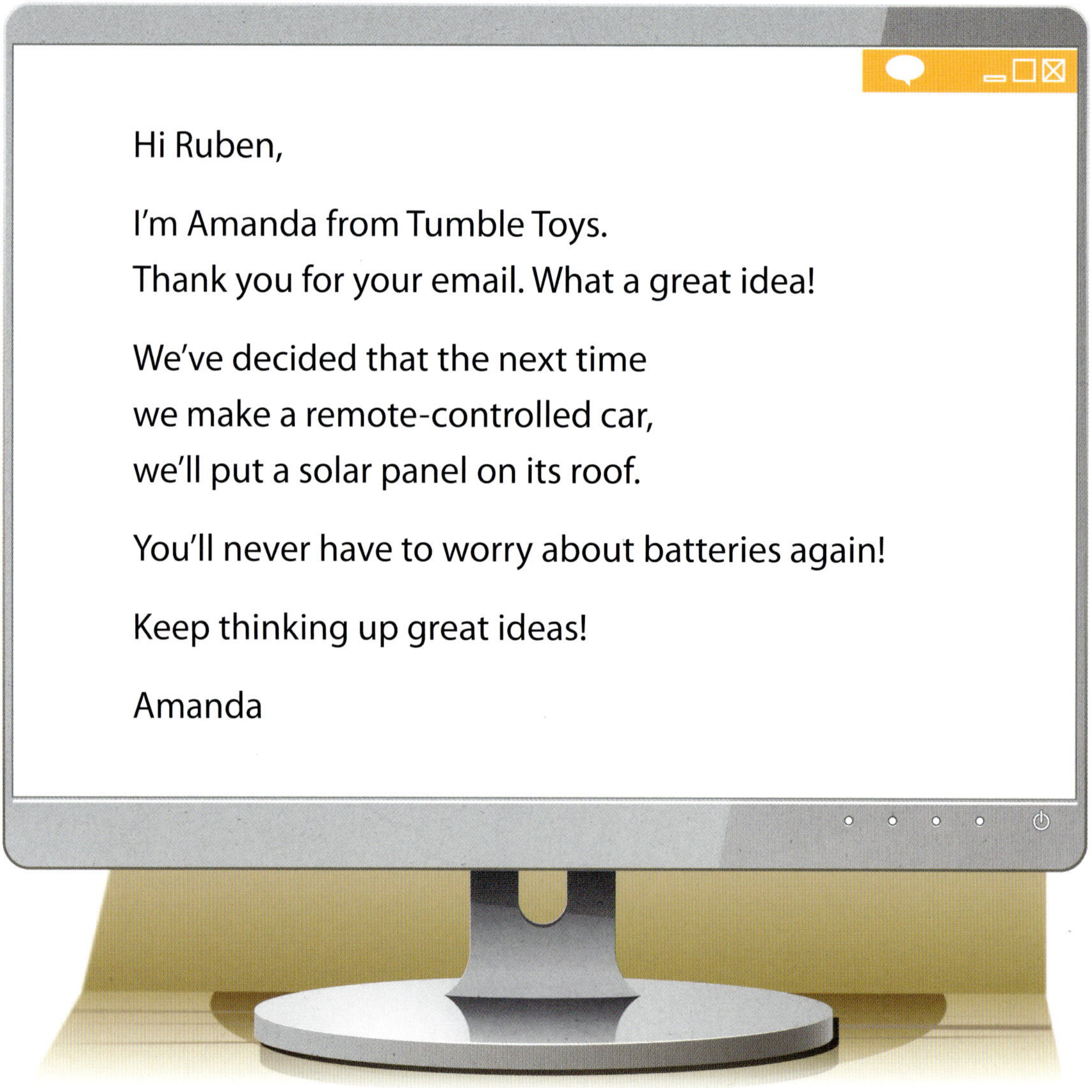

Hi Ruben,

I'm Amanda from Tumble Toys.
Thank you for your email. What a great idea!

We've decided that the next time
we make a remote-controlled car,
we'll put a solar panel on its roof.

You'll never have to worry about batteries again!

Keep thinking up great ideas!

Amanda

Ruben printed the email and took it to school.

Mr Tamura, Max and Ruben's other friends were very excited about it.

Chapter 4

A Speedy Surprise

A few weeks later, Ruben was eating breakfast when someone knocked on the door.
Mum opened the door, and Ruben heard a man say, "I have a box for Ruben Reed."

Mum brought the box inside and put it down
on the kitchen table.
Anxiously, Ruben opened it.

Inside, there was something covered in crumpled paper.
Carefully, Ruben lifted the paper.
He could hardly believe his eyes.

It was a remote-controlled car that looked
just like his old ones,
but with a glistening solar panel on its roof!

"Look at this, Mum!" cried Ruben,
taking the car out of the box. "It's magnificent!"

"And look at the side of the car!" said Mum.

Ruben lifted the car up and saw two words on the door: *Ruben Racer*.

He could hardly wait to show Mr Tamura and his friends at school!